I0624413

The Water Guardian
A Nexus Chronicle

The Water Guardian
A Nexus Chronicle

Mhairi Simpson

www.skytintbooks.co.uk

The Water Guardian © Mhairi Simpson 2014

Cover design by Mhairi Simpson.
Images used:
© Cattallina | Dreamstime.com - Dragon vector
© Sdecoret | Dreamstime.com - Red nebula over the
planet Earth

ISBN-13: 978-1-910658-12-3
ISBN-10: 1910658-12-X

SkyTint Books
www.skytintbooks.co.uk
mhairi@skytintbooks.co.uk

For Amanda, Lady L, Mel, Ren and Sarah
every time I fall in the water, you pull me out.

The Water Guardian

In the beginning, there was the One. Then there was Thought, and the First Thought was BALANCE. The Second Thought was LIGHT and there was Ylrith, the bringer of light. To balance the light there was Mahweh, the bringer of darkness.

Ylrith and Mahweh, the First Gods, saw that they were different and they argued over who was the greatest. The One laughed and told them that where one was, so must the other be. That was the nature of Balance and the balance of Nature.

But there was also the Other. The Other's First Thought was its only thought – POWER.

- The First Thoughts
as told to supplicants at the Great Oak near Lirios

The Third Thought was COMPASSION and there was the Lord Guardian, defender of the weak, voice of the mute.

Ylrith and Mahweh, the First Gods, saw the Lord Guardian, pure compassion, gentle and kind, and asked the One, "How can this be? Where is the balance?" The One thought on this and realised it could not be. Then he was troubled, for balance should occur of itself and yet none had come forth.

The Other called from his lands in the aether, whispering on the wind. "He shall be the most powerful creature in this or any other world," he said. As he spoke, the Lord Guardian grew great fangs, an impenetrable hide and became the fastest, strongest creature on the land, in the air or under the water.

The One saw that his new creation was balanced and it was good.
The Other only smiled.

- The Creation of the First Guardian
from the Glass History, housed at the Shattered Elm in
Coria (The Rose City)

Ranya waited for a break in the flow of people, then stepped out the door, head held high. Not that it did her any good. At six cycles, and small for her age, she barely reached the lower shoulder on most adults. But she had to look as though she knew where she was going. Her parents were down at the waterfront, part of the escort for the review of the Ambassador's ship prior to the Scion and her family leaving the Rose City and returning to Water. As long as no one decided she looked lost, she had several hours before her parents returned home.

She turned towards the waterfront, but pulled up short at the scuffle ahead of her on the Water side of the street.

A cluster of half a dozen boys pushed and kicked at something on the ground. Ranya swallowed. She didn't want to cross the street just yet, but she knew one of those boys. The emblem outlined in turquoise thread on his jerkin was unmistakeable. She had no wish whatsoever to cross Theron, not today. Not ever.

The boys moved and she saw a shape on the ground. As she watched, a hand latched around Theron's ankle and he hit the ground with a yell. In the gap, she saw a boy, arms flailing, two or three hands punching or grabbing as he kept one arm, sometimes two, over his face to protect it.

Ranya sighed.

She didn't get the whole 'them and us' thing between Tovarikin and Varika. As a Varik, one with the ability to manipulate the element of water, she was supposed to be superior to the four-armed Tovarikin, but there had been numerous occasions when she had strongly wished for a second pair of hands. Particularly as her elemental ability was barely enough to corral drops on a plate.

A prehensile tail whipped around another boy's ankle and he screamed as his leg went out from under him. Ranya giggled. She wouldn't have minded a tail, either. She shifted her shoulders. The extra shoulder blades were a reminder that Tovarikin and Varika were all born alike. Any physical differences were down to the midwife's blade.

The Tovarik was scrambling to his feet. Theron watched from the dust, his face a mask of hate, but then his expression changed, his lips widening in a smile, as water boiled up from a bucket next to a pastry stall and shot straight towards the back of the Tovarik's head.

Ranya screamed a warning, already running towards them as the wordless cry left her lips, and the Tovarik turned and ducked, but not quickly enough. Water engulfed his head. He clawed at his face, falling to his knees. The Varika watched and laughed, occasionally kicking him.

Ranya looked around desperately. Her eyes lit on a loose stone and she wondered if she dared. Through the circle of Varika, she saw the Tovarik writhing on his back, drowning on dry land. She had no choice. She picked up the stone and threw it with all her strength.

All her strength turned out to be more than enough. The cobble flew, straight and true, striking Theron neatly in the back of the head. He fell across the Tovarik's legs, and the tov turned his head, coughing up water, then punched Theron firmly in the face before pushing himself unsteadily to his feet. He leapt out of the circle of boys, across the street and down an alley. The other Varika were so shocked by Theron's collapse they mustered water too late. He was gone from sight before the bubbles could reach him and the water splashed to the ground as they turned to see Ranya, turning red with the realisation of what she'd done.

Theron threw off the Varik attempting to help him up.

"What the fuck happened?" he snarled, then followed the direction one of his friends was pointing - Ranya. Their eyes locked. She turned and ran.

She ducked behind a sausage seller's stall, but ran again after catching sight of the flicker of fear in the man's face. She didn't blame him for not wanting to get involved. Theron's family emblem was well known. No one wanted to get in trouble with the Ambassador's family, even if he was a fairly distant cousin.

She dived down an alley on the Tovarik side of the Line, knowing her only hope was to stay out of sight. Shouts behind her and pounding feet alerted her to a couple of facts. One, they weren't going to let her get away as easily as the

Tovarik boy, and two, they were all several years older than her, with correspondingly longer legs.

She twisted and turned, down alleyways, onto the Line and back off again. She saw her destination and risked an all-out run. Something cold and wet smacked into the back of her neck and started crawling around towards her mouth and nose. She didn't waste time trying to push it away, just ran faster, even though her legs burned and her lungs were exploding. The water reached her tightly closed lips, before rushing upwards into her nose. She hit the door hard, her weight pushing it open, and she fell on the floor, gasping and choking as the water crowded down into her lungs. The door swung shut behind her and the water ceased its attack, the energy directing it cut off as the door hid her from the wielder's sight. She turned over and coughed and coughed until the floor was soaked and she could breathe again.

Light globes cast a steady light and soft shadows around the shopfloor, but the man beside her blocked it out. She realised he was holding her head and body, supporting her while she retched up the water. A third hand offered a towel which she took to dry her face off and the fourth was braced against the floor, supporting his upper body.

"Upsetting your people again, Ranya?" Tomin's voice was low, gentle. She'd never seen him angry. He didn't seem to mind that she was Varik, either. She sat up and he let her go, squatting back on his heels.

"They were hurting a tov," she said, then winced. "I mean, a Tovarik. They were using Water on him. It wasn't fair. There was only one of him, and he didn't have an element."

"Indeed." He stood up and moved away towards the back of the shop. "And what did you do?"

"I yelled to warn the boy of the water. And then I…"

Tomin turned at her hesitation.

"Yes?"

"I threw a stone at Theron's head," Ranya murmured. If her father found out, she'd be in so much trouble. She'd never be allowed out of the house on her own again. Her worries were interrupted by a roll of thunder from the back of the shop. She looked up in surprise.

Tomin was laughing, bracing his lower fists on his knees to hold himself up while his upper arms wrapped around his ribs as though they ached. Eventually he straightened and wiped his eyes, still chortling.

"Ah, Ranya, one day you will be a leader of men. Here…" he reached up onto a shelf and took down a small wooden box. "This is for you."

She sidled towards him. Tomin let her play with many of the tech devices in his shop, but he'd never given her any of them. The light in the globes set at regular intervals around the walls lit his face, open and kind, without a flicker. Tovarik light wasn't produced with fire. Any member of that House could turn that off and on as they pleased. Technically, a member of Ranya's own House, Water, would also be able to dowse them at will. Neither possibility was desirable to a Tov, a non-magical individual born without the ability to manipulate one of the five elements. Ranya stood on tiptoe, craning to see the box.

Tomin grinned, crouching down before opening it. Ranya was already leaning forward as the lid rose and she started back, thrown by the soft light that glowed within. The lid closed and Tomin's big, nimble fingers lifted a tiny hook to keep it secure before holding the box out to her.

"For you, my Lady of Water."

She stared up at him. Then shame washed over her cheeks, and she looked down at her feet as tears filled her eyes.

"It's beautiful, but… I have no money, Mil Tomin."

A finger under her chin forced her to look him in the eye. He held the box out to her again.

"Kindness is its own guide, but sometimes it helps to have a little extra light on the matter. If it fades, leave it outside when the moon is out, or better still, during a storm. It will be as bright as ever within a few hours." He stood back and crossed his arms. She hesitated still and he glared. "Go! Do you want your father to come looking for you?"

She flinched and ran, but not before carefully peeking out the door to make sure Theron and his gang were gone. They'd probably thought she would be reamed for throwing herself bodily into some tov's shop and gone happily on their way.

The sector line was busier now, the wide road more than half filled with vendors calling to customers, customers ignoring vendors, dusty travellers heading towards the Palace Mount and clean travellers heading away from it. And everywhere, between human and *kelith* legs, scampered children and *coolran* and *dilin* in a medley of chubby skin, fur, scales and whiskers.

Ranya looked across the Line to her family's home. Technically, she hadn't done anything wrong in sneaking out. But the fact she'd had to sneak out told its own story. A booming *screar*, as though the sky itself screamed, came from the waterfront. You could tell those who didn't live in the city. They were the ones who flinched at the Guardians' calls.

The Water Guardian was calling to the Scion. She smiled. Their calls always made her smile. Even though Ranya's family lived quite a way from the waterfront and she had never actually seen a Water Guardian with her own eyes, their calls reassured her, made her feel safe. There was no logic to it at all. They couldn't give her greater power over her element, even if she did meet one. She clutched the small box in her hand, straightened her spine, and walked calmly across the road to her home.

She paused for a moment at the door to run her fingers over the image of a Water Guardian, picked out in coloured glass. A long, snakelike body coiled across the panel, delicate sails too large to be called fins curving gracefully out on either side. The Water Guardian's head spoke of power, even in tiny pieces of glass, eyes glowing gold, mouth agape to show curving fangs. Horns speared back from the rear of its head, which was shaped very much like a horse's but for the huge teeth and scaled skin.

The look on Kelian's face when Ranya entered the kitchen reminded her of the mad run through the alleyways of the tov sector on the other side of the Line, falling into Tomin's shop and throwing up all over the floor. She bit her lip. Kelian shot a worried gaze at Celith, who rolled her eyes.

"Get her changed, now! If her father sees her like that…" She didn't need to complete the sentence. Kelian grabbed Ranya's arm, hustling her through the house and up to her room. She called water up through the heated pipes and it splashed, steaming, into the big, caulked, wooden bath.

"Mmmm," sighed Ranya as Kelian lifted her into the bath and the water covered her, warming her through after the excitement of the morning.

"You're not supposed to be enjoying yourself, you know," Kelian told her, as she scrubbed her back and Ranya ran a cloth over her arms and face.

"But it's nice and warm," Ranya pointed out, and Kelian smiled, then shook her head and got back to work. Ranya smiled too. Kelian only smiled when she knew no one would tell Ranya's father. Ranya liked to see her smile.

***

Having dinner with the Scion wasn't nearly as exciting as everyone acted like it should be. The room was so big that after the initial introduction she couldn't even see the Scion any more, and everyone was shouting and it was really hot. The puffy dress with lots and lots of underskirts that her mother had insisted she wear was totally unlike what she normally wore. It made her feel cramped and uncomfortable.

A droplet of water landed on her face and she giggled, looking up at the live water sculpture that constantly swirled, dividing and rejoining in the huge hall, high above everyone's heads. In each corner of the room stood a man or a woman, two of each in total, dressed in robes of every shade of blue. Their eyes never left the water that flowed through the air, catching the light from hundreds of light globes and casting it around the room in rainbows. Hardly anyone was watching, which Ranya couldn't understand, but in a way that made it more special. Like the display was just for her.

Her father's guffawing laughter caught her attention. His cheeks were red and he was sweating. His eyes had that faraway look he got when he'd drunk a lot of wine. Ranya usually took that as her cue to slip away to her room. There were so many people here, she wasn't sure it was a good idea, though. Surely someone would notice?

She looked around. Everyone was talking to everyone else. She kicked her feet under the table. Even the lady directly opposite her was deep in conversation with a man to her right. She peeped sideways. Her father was laughing again, his hand inside her mother's dress. She bit her lip, stared at her mother-of-pearl plate, then came to a decision. The plate was shiny and full of pretty colours, but it had been pretty all night and she was still bored. Turning round, she slid down off the chair and walked quickly towards the nearest doorway.

The passageway was wide and well lit, and she dodged around a footman carrying a huge wooden platter. If it had been dessert she might have turned back, but it smelled meaty and she was already full, so she kept going.

The kitchen was huge and very busy. All Ranya could see was legs and waistcoats decorated with coral and tiny seashells, and larger shells for the buttons. It was very hot and very loud, with men and women shouting for pots, food, drink and cloths. For a moment she stood frozen in the passageway, then, realising she was going to get run over, ducked down to slide under a trolley.

The footmen were gliding out with platters and staggering back in with piles of empty plates. Ranya was going to have to move if she was to find a way out of the kitchen. It was just too big for her to see the doors from here. She pulled herself out from under the trolley and slid around the edges of the big room until she spotted an open doorway. She hurried towards it, then pulled up short as a man stepped right in front of her. She lifted her head, craning her neck right back to see his face. But he wasn't looking at her.

"Kreli! Where are the *cuksi*? You know what the Scion is like about her greens."

"Right here, Chef." Kreli, a thin-faced boy whose face was far lower than Chef's, looked confident as he handed Chef a large bowl.

"About time." Chef grabbed the bowl and turned away. Ranya sprinted for the door.

It was cool and dark outside, and she looked around the courtyard. The entrance was closed, but the postern gate was probably unlocked. She'd seen Kelian come in late through the postern gate at home. She skipped across the courtyard and tried the door. Sure enough, it opened, and she stepped out onto the street.

The moon blazed down, making the harbour waters sparkle like mother-of-pearl and Ranya ran towards the jetty. She hardly ever got to come down here. Everyone was always too busy. Well, they said they were, but she knew Father didn't like taking her out. People would ask what level she had and he'd have to tell them she was a o5. A Water elemental related to the Water Ambassador himself and only a o5? It made her sad too.

At the end of the jetty, she lay down on the wood and dipped her hand in the water, humming to herself. The tune the trumpets had played that afternoon was a pretty one, and she hummed it now, swirling her hand in the water and lifting it from time to time to see the drops fall from her fingers and catch the moonlight, like little pearls.

The water slapped against the ships and the jetty, but then the sound changed, and Ranya looked up to find the moon partly blocked out by a huge ship gliding past. She craned her head up and up and in the end had to sit up on the jetty in order to see properly. But her hands were wet and she put one on her skirt instead of the wood she was lying on to push herself up. Her hand shot sideways and the other hand clutched at nothing. Her scream was cut short as she fell head first into the water.

She couldn't see anything as water boiled around her, so she squeezed them shut. They stung horribly and she wanted to rub them while she fell, or was she? She couldn't tell which way was up, and when she breathed it wasn't air but water which rushed in through her nose and mouth. Her lungs burned and her body froze and she wanted to cry but couldn't make a sound. Was this what it felt like to die?

Something hit her belly and pushed. She fell against something hard and was suddenly even colder. A breeze whispered across her face, chilling her skin. She stretched out her fingers and her nails caught on the rough wood of the jetty. She coughed up water across the planks, gasping and writhing until finally she could breathe again.

Something nudged her hip and she moaned. It touched her hand this time, cold and wet, and her eyes flew open.

Moonlight outlined the Water Guardian's head and caught in the water dripping off its massive scaled snout and fangs as long as her arm. It was a dark shadow against the night sky, sails arching out from its head as it towered over her, even with most of its bulk hidden beneath the waters of the harbour. Its golden eyes glowed, though, the moon reflected in the dark, five-pointed star at the centre. The Guardian dropped its head and nudged her foot, one fang tearing a splintered gash in the jetty. She pulled her foot away, and then felt bad.

"Did you save me?" she asked. The Guardian put its head on one side, then lowered it to rest its chin on the jetty next to her, sails drooping alongside his neck. "You don't talk?"

His eyes flashed purple, then gold again. He sighed.

"You're young and you don't talk yet." Ranya knew what that was like. She was old enough to talk and people still acted like she couldn't. She reached out to stroke the scaly snout. "It must get lonely."

The Guardian angled his head, revealing smaller, softer scales under his chin, still silvered with water, and she took the hint, stroking lower down. His eyes closed and he sighed in appreciation. She shivered as the night breeze cut through her wet clothes, and felt like a terrible failure. She couldn't even dry her own clothes. Her shivers got stronger until her hand shook where it stroked over the Guardian's skin. The eyes snapped open.

He lifted his head and looked at her. She scrambled to her feet, wrapping her arms around herself. Had she done something to annoy him?

"I'm s-s-sorry," she stammered, cold making her teeth chatter. "It's the w-water, y-you s-see."

The Guardian opened its mouth and took a breath, then paused. Cocked his head. It looked like he was listening. Then he opened his mouth again and bugled, a high clear sound. It was like a question, but a call as well.

He lowered his head to her side and she leant against him. His scales were curiously warm to the touch, but this time a sail curved around to wrap her tightly against his head. She shrieked as it slid around her, silky soft, then realised what he was doing as she was enveloped in heat. She sighed and snuggled down.

***

She woke to find everything vibrating. Opening her eyes, she blinked blearily. It was a lot lighter now, but the Guardian still had her securely wrapped up next to his head. She was blissfully warm.

"Ranya?" Her father's voice snapped her fully awake. Her heart sank as he called her name again. She knew that tone and cringed away from it. The vibrations got stronger and now she heard a rumbling sound as well. It was the Guardian.

"Is that your daughter?" Ranya didn't recognise this new voice. Low. Calm. Female.

"I think so," said Mother.

Father's voice cracked out once more. "Ranya, come out of there!"

Ranya tried, but she was still held tight.

"It's okay," she whispered. "He's my father."

The vibrations deepened.

"Carathshiel," said the woman. "Release the child."

Carathshiel snorted but the sail unwound and Ranya stumbled before finding her feet. She shivered again and the Guardian's huge head pressed gently against her.

"Ranya."

Ranya's shoulders hunched, but she stepped forward towards her parents. She knew that tone. She was in so much trouble.

"The Guardian saved me, Father. I fell in the water and he picked me up and put me back on the wood."

He grabbed her hand and yanked her forward.

"And he wouldn't have had to if you had stayed in your seat as you ought!"

The next moment everyone ducked as Carathshiel reared up, his neck seeming to rise forever, cascading water over the jetty and the assemblage. Ranya almost fell over trying to crane her head far enough back to see him. His mouth gaped open, lips peeling back to reveal rows of glinting fangs. Then he roared.

Everyone clapped their hands over their ears, except the woman who had spoken. Ranya opened her eyes when she remembered she couldn't hear through them, and saw the woman standing tall amongst the courtiers. After a while Carathshiel fell silent, sliding back down into the water, lowering his head until he was nose to nose with Ranya's father.

In the distance, thunder rumbled, even though the sky was clear. Ranya felt her stomach turn over. Oroksharn had heard his subject's cry.

"I think, Varike Mestrien, that Carathshiel is angered."

Ranya felt her father's fingers clench tighter around her wrist.

"My apologies, Lord Guardian," he stammered.

Carathshiel snorted, blasting warm water across the jetty. Ranya tried not to smile. The Guardian might be young but he knew when he was being flattered. There was only one Lord Guardian, who might even now be on his way to investigate the source of his subject's distress.

"Come and see us tomorrow, Varike Mestrien," said the woman. "We would speak with you in calmer times. And bring your daughter." She looked down at Ranya and smiled. Ranya smiled back. "She intrigues us."

Her father made a choked sound before bowing low and backing away. Ranya tried to control her shivers, but as she turned away she was struck by a cold so severe it convulsed her and she nearly fell over. Her father yanked her upright, then remembered himself, his hands gentling. But Ranya was more interested in the fact that her clothes were now dry. She knew her father hadn't done it. She looked over her shoulder. The woman was still smiling.

Ranya waited for Father to start shouting, but he didn't, even when they were out of sight of the jetty. They walked between the buildings to the road. The moon reached down even into this street. Ranya tried to see Father's face but she could only see his cheek and the point of his nose.

They reached the Sector Line and turned towards the Palace. A large carriage stood in front of the building they had gone to dinner in, with eight light blue horses harnessed in front of it. Father guided them right up the side of the walker so they wouldn't upset the horses.

As they passed the carriage, the driver swung down and Ranya shrank away from the massive whip in his hand.

"Varike Mestrien?"

Father stopped. They all stared at the driver.

"Er, yes."

"The Scion gave instructions that I was to take you and your family home. It's late to be walking, even on a Sector Line."

Ranya looked up at her father. The knob in his throat bobbed as he swallowed.

"We'd be honoured to accept," he said, in a strange tone, flat and sad. The driver opened the door of the carriage and lifted Ranya up into the darkness. For a moment she was scared, but then her eyes adjusted and she could see cushions and the shape of the door on the other side. She pulled herself up onto the seat and sat facing the front of the carriage. She heard murmurs outside, then Mother and Father got in after her and sat down, Mother next to Ranya and Father opposite them. The door closed and the carriage dipped as the driver climbed up. A moment later there was a lurch and they started moving.

Ranya had never been in such a fine carriage before and soon she was on the edge of her seat, staring out the window at the buildings going by along the Sector Line. The line looked huge, the lack of people showing her how big it really was. She picked out where Mil Crovas had his fruit stall, and where Mili Nerkiden repaired shoes. When she saw the alleyway that led to Tomin's shop she knew they were nearly home, and she was a little sad. It was a lovely carriage.

When the carriage stopped, the driver got down and opened the door. Father got out and Mother handed Ranya into his arms. She was surprised. Usually they just left her to sort herself out. Of course, they'd never ridden in such a tall carriage before. And on top of that, she'd met and hugged a Water Guardian.

Her eyes were closing as Father carried her into her room and laid her on her bed. She blinked to see Kelian standing in the doorway, her hand over her mouth.

"Pick out her finest outfit," he said as he turned towards the door. "We visit the Scion on the morrow."

"The Scion? But, didn't you just—?" She cut herself off, as though only now remembering what happened when she questioned her employer, but Father didn't seem to notice.

"Yes, we did. But now she wants to meet Ranya. Properly." His voice was heavy as he left the room, walking like an old man.

Ranya knew she would never live a day as wonderful as today again. But then she thought of the warmth of Carathshiel's head, and she smiled.

***

The next morning, Ranya woke early, wondering if the night before had only been a dream. Maybe she'd fallen asleep at the table during the banquet and imagined everything else. She sat up in bed and opened the little box that sat on the windowsill. The light globe shone brightly and she grinned. At least that was real. She closed the box and threw back the quilts just as Kelian bustled in.

"Come along now, miss. We've lots to do and not a lot of time to do it in. Into the bath with you!" Ranya skipped into the bathroom while Kelian followed her, muttering about children who stayed up all night and didn't have the sense to know when the tide was going out.

"Why would I know if the tide was going out?" asked Ranya as she pulled her nightgown off.

Kelian's face went slack, then she pulled herself together and started *calling* the water into the bath.

"It's nothing to do with the tide, you must have heard me wrong," she said, in a voice Ranya didn't want to argue with. "Into the bath."

Ranya was soon standing in her room, pink and clean and dry, as Kelian put more clothes on her than she had ever worn before. They were all very fine, thin things though, so she barely felt the weight of them. She looked in the mirror and saw an outfit which looked quite a lot like the dress she'd worn last night, but had taken twice as long to put on.

"And now for the overdress," said Kelian. "Arms up."

Ranya lifted her arms and fabric slithered down over them.

"Oof," she said as the weight of the overdress settled around. She looked down and gasped.

Pearls and mother-of-pearl and tiny shells covered almost every inch of the fabric. Kelian was now buttoning the dress up the back and Ranya watched as the image in the mirror changed to someone who looked a lot older. And much more important.

She was still staring when Kelian straightened up. Their eyes met in the mirror.

"Whose dress is this?" Ranya whispered, running her palm over the skirt and feeling the pearls and shells tickle her hand.

"It's Veliu's."

Ranya nodded. Her memories of her eldest sister before she got married the year before were mostly of her spinning around the hall in beautiful dresses. Veliu loved gorgeous clothes. Ranya preferred things she could run around in. As a consequence, most of her dresses were worn around the hem. Not fit for the Scion at all. After all, she couldn't wear last night's dress again today and it was the best she had.

Kelian ran a hand over Ranya's hair.

"You're growing up fast, miss."

Ranya looked up at her. She had a feeling growing up wasn't something she really wanted to do.

"Oh!" Kelian was off across the room to a chest. She opened it up and took something out. "I nearly forgot the reticule. A lady needs something to put her bits in."

Ranya took the small bag, with its thin loop and turned it over in her hands. It matched her overdress precisely, with pearly gleaming thread coiling across it to describe a Water Guardian. The stitching was so fine it might have been Carathshiel, frozen as he reared out of the water to roar his displeasure, head and neck towering high.

Ranya skipped across to the windowsill, or tried to. The dress was heavier even than the one she'd worn the night before, forcing her to shuffle sedately. She was utterly defeated by her bed. Leaning was impossible. Tears sprang to her eyes as she reached and reached for the box, but the dress held her back.

Her lip was quivering when an arm reached over her and brought her the box.

"This what you're after, miss?" Kelian asked softly. Ranya nodded in silence, worried that if she tried to speak, tears might fall on the beautiful dress.

"I don't want to be grown up," she whispered. She felt a sliding pressure on her head. Kelian was stroking her hair.

"It's only for today, miss. Everything'll be back to normal by tonight."

Ranya opened the box and put the globe into her bag, then shuffled out of her room and was nearly defeated by the stairs.

"You go down sideways, miss, like this," Kelian reminded her. They went down the stairs together, like two crabs, one of which had fallen into a Metal's coining vat. Ranya was so focussed on getting down the stairs without falling down them that it didn't even seem funny.

Mother and Father were both dressed up in pearls and shells too, and breakfast was quiet. Ranya was afraid to eat anything in case she stained the dress and neither of her parents seemed to notice. Father finished sipping his chocolate and set his cup down. He took a breath, as though he were going to say something, but Mirik stepped into the room at that moment, his body very stiff, like a board.

"Varike Mestrien, there is a gentleman at the door saying he has been appointed to drive you, your Veriki and your daughter to the Scion's residence."

Father closed his mouth. Swallowed.

"We'd best be going, then."

Ranya slid down off her chair. She was starting to get nervous, clutching the reticule with the light globe in. She knew she'd done something wrong, she just couldn't work out why Father hadn't yelled at her for it.

"Come on, Ranya, don't dawdle." Father's voice bit and Ranya shrank a little. Suddenly the dress was very, very heavy indeed.

It hadn't been a dream and right then, all she could remember was Carathshiel's anger.

Mother reached down and grabbed her hand. The reticule slipped but Ranya grabbed it tight with her other hand and shuffled along as best she could, praying to the One that she wouldn't trip and upset her parents even more.

This time it was the driver who lifted her up into the carriage, and she had to wait until Mother got in to sit on the seats. She couldn't climb up in the dress. It was too tight and too stiff. And too bright. Her tummy rumbled and she squished it through the dress, hoping no one had heard. Neither Mother nor Father gave any sign they had.

"Do you think she is angered?" Mother asked. Ranya opened her mouth to ask who was angered, but Father replied first.

"I do not know. I know we are not her favourites, and the Guardian has already grown very protective of..." He trailed off as he looked at Ranya. He seemed surprised to find her looking back. "I believe she thinks well of Ranya. We will see. We have broken no laws. That is the main thing."

Mother sighed.

"There are laws, and there are Laws," she said, with careful emphasis. "I fear we may have been remiss in-"

"No!"

Ranya pressed herself back into the cushions as Father snapped the word.

"We have broken no laws." He looked at Ranya, and his eyes were cold. "If you had just stayed in your seat..."

Ranya stared at the reticule, running her fingers over the shape of the globe inside. It was all her fault. The Scion was angry, so Mother and Father were angry, and she shouldn't have left the table. Would she have seen the Water Guardian so close? Of course not.

It seemed only a moment later that the carriage stopped and the driver opened the door again. Ranya's heart dropped into her gurgling stomach. She was starting to feel quite sick.

They were led through corridors by footmen in the same every kind of blue uniform and finally arrived at a small room with a huge pair of doors at the other end. A man in a gorgeous uniform, every shade of green and blue covered with shapes cut from mother-of-pearl and coral, raised a staff made of a single piece of white coral and inlaid with pearls and mother-of-pearl and smaller pieces of brightly coloured coral and knocked on the doors with it.

Once.

Twice.

The doors opened from the inside and Father grabbed Ranya and pulled her in front of him.

"Enter," came the same warm voice Ranya remembered from the night before. Father gave her a little push and she walked forward.

The room on the other side of the doors was enormous, and Ranya immediately recognised it as the great hall they had had dinner in the night before. She looked around for the water sculpture and Father tapped her cheek to remind her to look forward. She blushed furiously and held her head high and straight all the rest of the way to the dais at the other end. The woman sitting in the throne was the same woman who had come to the jetty last night! The one who knew Carathshiel's name. Ranya realised with horror that she had already met the Scion of Water, second in power only to the Water Lord, and her face burned even hotter. She almost forgot to curtsey, but remembered after a moment and straightened again, rustling fabric behind her telling her that her parents were doing the same.

"We are pleased to welcome you to our house, Verikin Mestrien." The Scion looked no different. She was wearing very formal clothes, but her face was exactly the same.

Ranya heard more rustling behind her and realised she should have stayed curtsied until the Scion welcomed them. Her stomach turned over and she realised she was going to be sick. She looked around wildly for a bucket, a door,

31

something, but she was in a very big room and all eyes were on her.

"Ranya?"

At the sound of her name, Ranya looked up into the eyes of the Scion, all the way up at the top of the throne.

"I…I…" Ranya clapped her hand over her mouth.

"A bowl!" snapped the Scion, and a footman rushed forward, just in time for Ranya to throw up in the bowl. There wasn't much there, because she hadn't eaten, but she felt very strange now, all light and fluffy. She swayed. She could hear other voices now, but they seemed very far away…

Someone was holding her and sitting her in a chair.

"Bring food. Something light."

"Yes, my Lady."

Ranya blinked. The wall was stripy. The walls hadn't looked stripy when she came in. She moved her head, trying to get a closer look, and realised she was lying down. That wasn't the wall. It was the ceiling.

"Varike Mestrien."

"My Lady."

"Your daughter is of pure Water?"

"Yes, my Lady."

"Then why do you not show her the same regard you showed your other two daughters?"

"I… I do, I…"

Ranya's skin turned cold as she heard her father stumble over his words.

"In truth, my Lady, her lack of ability… I saw it as a shame on our family line. I had hoped she would grow to be more powerful, but it seems this will not happen. My *variki* and our daughters are embarrassed, and so am I."

"Embarrassed." The Scion's voice wasn't warm anymore. It was very like the sea now, full of cold depths. "Such a meaningful word, and yet, when applied to a child of six cycles, I find it hard to believe. You are aware, are you not, that the more powerful the ability, the longer it takes to surface?"

"My Lady?"

There was a very long silence.

***

Ranya stood on the deck of the ship, enjoying the feel of the wind whipping through her hair and the smooth scales of Carathshiel's cheek beneath her palm as he leaned over the rail beside her. His great golden eyes constantly swept the deck, his neck disappearing into the waters of the harbour which hid his massive body. Ranya had searched through the crowds of people gathered at the dockside to see the Scion's ship leave, but couldn't see anyone she recognised. She wouldn't cry. She would have liked to see Kelian before she left. The Scion had asked if she would miss anyone, and she'd told her, but Kelian was obviously busy.

"All aboard!"

"All aboard!"

Carathshiel nudged her gently, then lifted his head off the railing and slid beneath the water. She watched him pass between the ship and the dock and head into the open waters of the harbour, then she turned back to the city.

It was a huge city, and yet she had seen hardly any of it. As she thought of Tomin's shop, she knew she would miss him too. Not Mother or Father, though. She hadn't really spent enough time with them ever to miss them. Thinking of Tomin, she drew the light globe out of the little bag. The sun caught it, making it glimmer and gleam, and an answering glimmer caught her attention in the crowd.

She grinned. Tomin stood there, cradling a ball of light in one hand. He raised another hand and waved. She waved back.

"Saying goodbye to your friend?" The Scion's voice was warm again, and Ranya nodded.

"Yes. I'll miss him."

"And your other friend, that you told me you would miss?"

"Kelian. She isn't here. I think she's busy. She has a lot of work to do."

"I work somewhere else now, miss."

Ranya turned, her smile nearly cracking her cheeks as she threw herself forward and into Kelian's arms.

"Where do you work now?"

"Where you live, miss. I'm your servant. The Scion, if it please your Lady," she curtsied, "bought my freedom from your parents. So we'll travel together, how's that?"

"As long as you don't make me wear that dress again," said Ranya, doing her best pout.

Kelian laughed and was about to answer when Carathshiel shot out of the water on the dockside of the ship. Higher and higher he rose, until he blocked out the sun, a curving tower of scaled muscle, then he arched over the ship, water sheeting down to drench all who stood below, and plummeted into the sea on the other side. Spray exploded and covered Ranya, Kelian and the Scion, along with half the ship's crew.

Kelian *called* the moisture from their clothes, including those of the Scion.

"Begging your pardon, my Lady," she excused herself, blushing mightily. "I know you can do it yourself, but I haven't got the control, you see. I'm terribly sorry."

"That's quite alright, Kelian. I need to go and talk to the captain anyway, and it's best to do so in dry clothing. Why don't you two stay here and enjoy the view?"

Ranya beamed and then waved to Carathshiel who reared up and roared his approval. This was going to be a wonderful trip.

Thank You

I'm so glad you decided to pick up this story and I hope you enjoyed it. If you did (or even if you didn't!) please consider writing a review, or even just telling your friends, so that they can benefit too.

Also, if you enjoyed the story and would like to read more of my work, you can find a list of my published work on my website, **www.mhairisimpson.com**. You can also sign up there for my new releases mailing list if you'd like to be among the first to know when I'm going to have a new release out. It's strictly for telling you about upcoming releases and giving you the option to get the newest story before anyone else.

If you'd like to contact me, please do! You can email me at **mhairi@mhairisimpson.com**. I look forward to hearing from you!

Acknowledgements

I owe a great debt to S. J. Higbee, without whose diligence this story would be much weaker. Kait, Ren and Leona have always been there for me, most of all when most sane people would stay away! And Adele, Susan, Kait, Amanda and Caroline are just the perfect enablers - I'd follow my dreams regardless but maybe not with so much laughter and grinning! I love you guys - thank you.

About The Author

Mhairi Simpson is a fantasy writer (mostly blood and inner demons) and inveterate traveller (mostly Europe and South America). An only child who grew up in boarding schools and with a background in modern languages and paper pushing, Mhairi has spent most of her life with words on a page, leading her to realise her best shot at faking sanity is to be a full time author/editor. She is most effectively bribed/tamed/friended with chocolate.

Find her online at:
Her website, Reality Refugee: http://mhairisimpson.com
Twitter: http://twitter.com/AMhairiSimpson
Facebook:
http://www.facebook.com/MhairiSimpsonAuthor